DO YOU LOVE ME?

STORY AND PICTURES BY DICK GACKENBACH

A YEARLING BOOK

Published by
Dell Publishing Co., Inc.
1 Dag Hammarskjold Plaza
New York, New York 10017

ISBN: 0-440-42067-9

Reprinted by arrangement with The Seabury Press, Inc.
Printed in the United States of America
First Yearling printing—March 1978

YEARLING BOOKS are designed especially to entertain and enlighten young people. The finest available books for children have been selected under the direction of Charles F. Reasoner, Professor of Elementary Education, New York University.

For a complete listing of all Yearling titles,
write to Education Sales Department, Dell Publishing Co., Inc.,
1 Dag Hammarskjold Plaza, New York, N.Y. 10017.

For Louise Fitzhugh

Walter liked breakfast because the family was all together and the kitchen smelled of warm biscuits, honey, and hot coffee. If he could have had his way, everyone would have stayed around that big table all morning, just laughing and talking. But Walter knew breakfast was over when Mr. Becker pushed his chair back from the table.

"Now don't you bother the cow or pester the pigs, Walter."

"No, Daddy," replied Walter, for he was learning that farm animals were not to play with.

"You're my pal," said his father as he left to work in the potato field.

Mrs. Becker sipped the last of her coffee. "I better start making up the beds," she said. "What are you going to do with yourself today, Walter?"

"Don't know yet, Momma."

"Well, stay out of trouble," Mrs. Becker said as she went up the back stairs.

Walter sat quietly with his sister Boots, listening to the sound of their mother's footsteps on the wooden floor above them. He was sorry breakfast was over. It was quarter past six and the day had begun.

"Maybe something special will happen today, Boots!" he said hopefully. "Maybe we'll get company."

"I doubt it." Boots got up from the table. "Now outside," she said firmly, "I've got to do the dishes."

"Can't I help?" Walter asked.

"Nope," said Boots. "You scrape up the biscuit crumbs and go feed your bugs and turtle."

Walter brushed every crumb from the checkered oilcloth into his cupped hand. "See you later, Boots," he said.

"See you later," she answered, "and don't slam the screen door!"

Too late! The screen door closed with Walter's usual *BANG*.

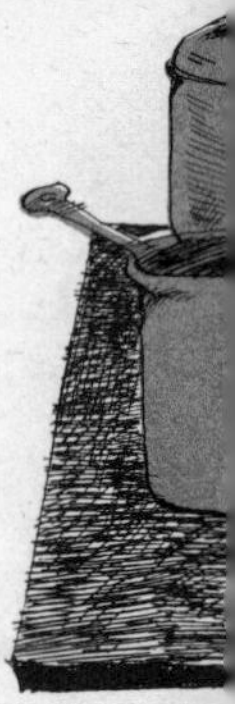

It was a bright morning. Walter stopped by the pump to fill an old tin can with water for his bugs and turtle.

While he was pumping on the handle, something green and shiny caught his eye. It was far away and over the flower garden. It was there for only a second and then it was gone.

"Could have been a dragonfly!" Walter said.

Suddenly the green dot appeared again. It moved like a bouncing ball over the flowers. Walter tried to shield his eyes from the morning sun to see better. Whatever it was, it was very fast and had disappeared again.

"Must have been a butterfly," he decided.

With his breakfast crumbs in one hand and the tin of water in the other, Walter hurried to the barn. His friends, the bugs and turtle, were waiting.

Walter enjoyed going to the big barn early in the morning. The doors were left open on summer nights, so the hay was still wet with dew, the morning mist still curled in the corners. There was a pleasant odor of damp dirt and damp hay and chicken feed.

On a shelf, next to cans of axle grease, Walter kept a jar of ants, and a jar of fireflies, and a turtle in an old shoebox. He was very fond of them, they belonged to him alone.

"Morning, bugs," he said, dropping the breakfast crumbs into the jars.

"Morning, turtle," he said, taking off the lid of the old shoebox. "I brought you something." He sprinkled the turtle's share of the biscuit crumbs into the box.

Walter picked up the turtle and held him against his cheek, but the turtle pulled back into his shell.

Walter kissed the turtle on his shell anyway and put him back into his box.

“Look out pigs! Here I come,” Walter yelled, leaning over the pig pen. The pigs were still sleeping and would most likely stay that way until Boots came to feed them. “Lazy pigs,” said Walter.

The rays of the early morning sun were coming through the window by the cow stall and Walter could see the flies were already beginning to trouble the cow.

"Shoo, shoo!" cried Walter, chasing the flies from her eyes.

"You should say thank you," he whispered into the cow's ear. But the cow just continued to chew on her hay.

Walter left the barn. The sun had already begun to dry the dew from the grass.

"What will I do today?" he wondered.

The family would be busy with chores all day and have no time to spend with him. Walter was still too small to be of help around the farm.

He often wished he had a friend to play with, but the nearest playmates were eight miles away. He could never walk that far, and his father could not afford to use the family car for such a trip.

So Walter had to make up his own games, and he was good at it.

"Guess I'll go count cars," he decided.

He ran to the front of the house, straddled the railing on the big porch, and waited for the first car to go by.

Counting cars was one of his favorite games. Even though Walter was only six, he knew the name of every car on the road.

"Here comes one!" he said. He studied the car as it came up the road.

"It's a Packard," he shouted. This was his lucky day, for a big Packard was a rare sight on an old dirt road like his.

"Hello!" he yelled as the Packard went by.

Walter waved, and the people in the car waved back and tooted their horn for him.

"That's some horn," he said, as he watched the Packard disappear down the road in a trail of dust.

"Well, that's number one," he said. "Hope number two is a Chevy." He settled down to wait for the next car.

Out in front of the house, alongside the road, stood a big yellow mailbox. It was by this mailbox that Walter saw the hummingbird.

He heard the bird before he saw her, just a whisper of a hum. His eyes searched for the humming sound —and there she was! She was the size of a large bee, and she was bobbing like a yo-yo in front of the box.

"That must have been what I saw in the garden," Walter realized.

The bird's feathers shone like emeralds and her wings beat so fast that they looked like a smudge on the air.

Walter could tell it was the rapid movement of her wings that caused the humming sound.

He watched the bird as she dangled completely still in mid-air. Walter never knew a bird could hover so, but this one did. The fast flutter of her wings made it possible.

He watched her as she flew backward to look into the mailbox. Walter was amazed, for he never knew a bird could fly backward, either.

He watched as she flew into the mailbox and out again in seconds. He had never seen a bird fly so fast.

He watched her fly away, across the road and into the field. She didn't fly like any other bird, her flight made dots and dashes across the sky. Then she was gone.

"Zowie!" Walter cried. "That bird was so tiny I could've put it in my pocket."

Walter liked that idea very much. "If only I could catch it," he thought, "I could take it everywhere with me. I could talk to it, I could pet it, and it would be my friend always."

"But how can I catch a bird that fast?" he asked himself. "I wonder what it was doing in the mailbox?"

Walter jumped from the porch, ran to the box, and looked inside. He saw the beginning of a tiny nest.

If the bird was making a nest, she would surely be back.

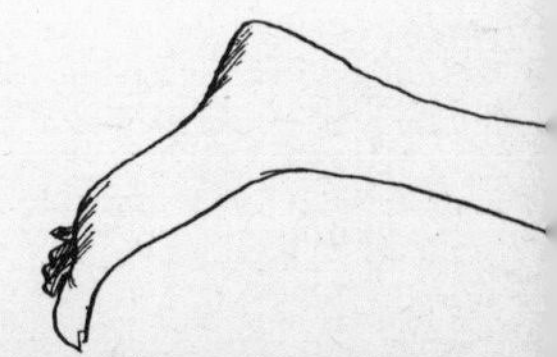

Walter hid behind a lilac bush and waited for the bird to return. It didn't take long.

He soon saw her coming back across the field. She was flying in that same crazy way, darting from one wildflower to another. Her slender beak was full of plant down to add to her nest.

When she entered the mailbox, Walter jumped from behind the lilac bush to slam the door shut and catch her.

The bird saw Walter jump. She became confused and frightened and flew toward the closing door. The door closed on her as she was coming through.

Walter pulled his hand away from the door, but it was too late. The bird dropped to the ground at his feet.

US MAIL

Walter picked her up and began to pet her, but she didn't move. She didn't sing or wiggle or even look up at him.

He knew something was wrong.

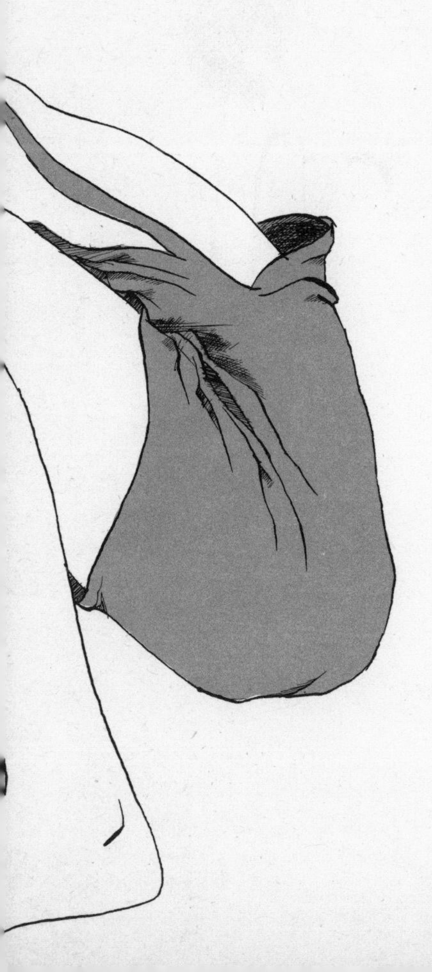

He was frightened.

"Please bird, be all right," he pleaded.

"What should I do?" he asked, as he looked at her. He would have done anything to make the bird right again.

Suddenly Walter thought of his sister. "Boots will fix her!" She had mended many birds that had flown into a window pane or fallen from a tree.

Boots was in the kitchen finishing the dishes when Walter burst through the door holding the little bird in his hand.

"Boots, Boots, fix the bird, please fix the bird."

But Boots knew as soon as she saw the bird that there was no fixing to be done. The hummingbird was dead.

"What happened?" asked Boots, her fingers lightly touching the bird.

"I tried to catch her, I only wanted to pet her," replied Walter, still sobbing.

"Poor little guy," Boots said as she wiped his face. "It was meant to be free, you should have let it be."

"I loved it, Boots," he said, his eyes red from crying. "I didn't mean to hurt it."

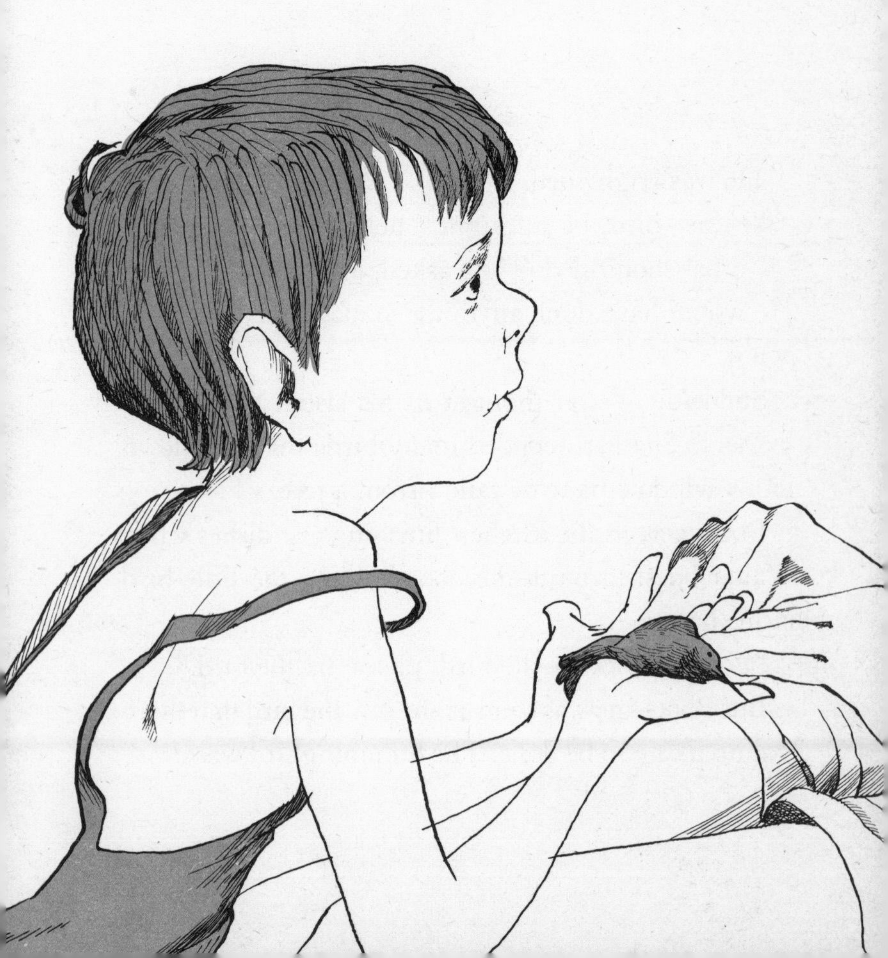

"I know you didn't," Boots assured him. "But how would you like it if some giant bird came swooping down from the sky and picked you up and kept petting you with a giant claw, even if it did love you? Huh, how'd you like that?"

Walter thought about that and decided he wouldn't like it.

"Not all creatures want you to love them," Boots continued. "Different creatures want different things from you."

"How can you tell who wants what?" asked Walter.

"Try a little respect first," Boots said. "Then wait and see what they want. You'll find out soon enough."

Walter buried the bird in the nicest part of the garden. He dug a hole, put her in, and covered her with dirt. Then he found a big white stone and put it on top of the dirt so that nothing could dig her up. When he was finished he sat down by the grave. He made a vow, then, never to try to catch a bird again.

The morning was almost over and Walter had no heart to make up any more games. He sat in the shade of the big apple tree and thought about the advice his sister had given him. He made up his mind to give it a try.

Walter went to the barn where he kept his ants and his fireflies and his turtle. He looked closely at the jars and asked, "Do you love me, bugs?" Then he opened the jars and one by one the ants crawled away and the fireflies flew away.

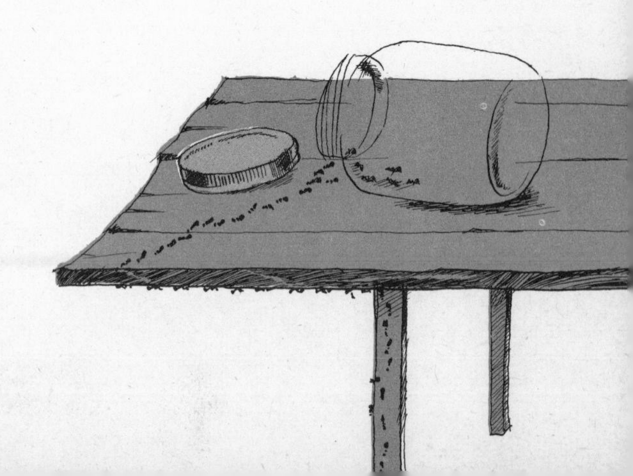

He opened the box with the turtle in it. "How about you, turtle?" he asked. He put the turtle on the ground and it crawled away as fast as a turtle can.

Walter had shown them respect and they had let him know they wanted their freedom.

Walter grabbed a handful of chicken feed and gave it to the chickens. The chickens ate the grain and walked away. They had shown Walter what they wanted.

"Dumb chickens don't love anybody," he said. "Hope we have you for Sunday dinner."

"Walter, Walter!" His mother was leaning out the kitchen window. "Call Daddy and Boots, tell them lunch is almost ready."

"Yes, Momma," yelled Walter. He knew his father was in the potato field, but he didn't know where Boots had gone.

Walter ran to the stone fence by the road and climbed on top of it. He waved to his father in the field. It was their signal. When his father saw Walter waving, he knew it was time to come for lunch.

While Walter was waving his father in from the field, he saw Boots walking up the road. "Hi," he called, as he ran down the road to meet her. "Where you been?"

Boots just looked at him and smiled as she reached inside her jacket and pulled out a small pup.

"I walked all the way down to Doc Raymer's place for this mutt," she said. "I knew his dog had pups and he'd be glad to get rid of one. Here! Take her and you better be good to her."

Walter took the pup from Boots, but he was terrified. He was afraid he'd hurt her the way he had hurt the hummingbird. He held the pup as gently as he held the Christmas balls when the family trimmed the tree.

"I'll be good to her, Boots," he promised.

Then he held the pup up close to his face and whispered so that Boots couldn't hear, "Do you love me?"

The pup nipped him lightly on his nose and licked his face.

That afternoon was one of the best in Walter's life. He and the pup ran together and played together and Walter wasn't lonesome again.

In the evening, when the family was able to gather around the radio and relax, Walter sat on the floor with his new friend.

"What are you going to call her?" asked his mother.

Walter stood up and thought for a while. Then he looked out the dark window toward the garden where he had buried the hummingbird.

"Bird," he said. "I'll call her Bird."

"That's a funny name for a dog," remarked his mother.

"Call her what you like, it's your dog," said his father.

“I think it’s a beautiful name,” said his sister Boots.